Ta

Grizzly Cove

All About
the Bear

BIANCA D'ARC

Copyright © 2015 Bianca D'Arc
All rights reserved.
ISBN: 1530284244
ISBN-13: 978-1530284245

DEDICATION

With heartfelt thanks to Jessica Bimberg, the first editor to see value in my work, way back in 2005. I'm so happy to be working with you again, Jess!

And, as always, to my family, who continue to make allowances for the crazy writer in their midst. I couldn't do it without your love and support.

PROLOGUE

"You want us to what?"

The question came from Brody, one of the highest ranked of John's lieutenants. If he couldn't convince Brody of the genius of his idea, he'd never have a shot at convincing the rest.

"We're going to pretend we're an artists' colony. That's the most sensible way we can fly under the radar around here." He'd researched it, and it was the only plan that made sense for this part of the country.

"But none of us are artists," Brody insisted.

"You can use a chainsaw, can't you?" He pointed at Brody, then went around the circle of his top men who were all gathered to hear the latest mission plan. "We all know Drew whittles in his spare time. And Sven can carve ice. Remember the swan he made

1

when we were undercover as caterers that time?"

"Tell me it's the fucking polar bear that came up with this," Peter the Russian shot a disgusted look at Sven, who flipped him the bird casually as he sat back to listen. Sven could always be counted on to listen first before jumping to conclusions.

As Alpha of this team of misfits, John had his work cut out for him, but he wouldn't have it any other way. All bear shifters, they'd bonded together over years of covert missions and top-secret assignments. And now, when the world had gone to hell and it was time to regroup, John had finally put his long-term plan into motion.

He'd been quietly buying up a huge tract of land near the very tip of Washington State over the past several decades. Every spare dollar he'd ever earned had gone into the project. He considered it an investment, and now that he had finally revealed his master plan to his men, he hoped they would take a more active role in buying up the rest of the land that they needed.

It was wild country with few inhabitants, yet the city wasn't too far away as the crow flies. And there were humans nearby. An Indian reservation and other coastal communities. If John and his team set up house here, they'd have to come up with a plausible cover story as to why there was suddenly a new settlement made up mostly of men in this remote area.

John had a plan to even out the numbers, too, but they'd have to be in residence first before he could put out the call through the shifter community to invite female bears who were looking for a change—and possibly a mate—to join them. There would probably be a few humans passing through on occasion, so they really needed that good cover story for their little community.

John laid out the long-term plan for them all for the first time, and thankfully, they listened. Bears were tricky. Most liked to roam alone, only settling down with a mate and raising their family much later in life—if at all. And they usually didn't live in such close proximity to their Alpha, which was more a ceremonial title than an actual authoritative one.

But John had been commanding officer to every one of the men who gathered around him at one time or another, and the role of leadership fell naturally to him. He might not be the biggest bear in the group, but he was universally believed to be the smartest when it came to strategy. He had hope for his people that they seemed to understand. He wanted to see these men, who had given so much of themselves to help protect the innocent, have fulfilling lives of their own now that they were retiring from the human world and its troubles.

Things had changed drastically in the shifter community. Dark times had accelerated John's plans for his men, but though they remained poised to help, the greater war seemed to be in a lull at the moment. Which left the bears at loose ends. That was why John had brought them all here, to Washington State, to lay the base for what he hoped would be a community that would last for generations.

It was a social experiment the likes of which had never really been attempted in the modern age. At least not on this scale. But if anyone could do it, John knew his men could. Bears were both strong and patient.

It took some doing, but eventually, he talked them all around, and they started planning in earnest for the settlement they were going to build. The community of Grizzly Cove would soon be a reality.

CHAPTER ONE

Brody walked along Main Street, marveling at the way the men had risen to the challenge when John set out the parameters for this new mission. They had drafted in a bit of help from the Clan of shifters that had their own construction company in Nevada, to plan and build the small town square. Other than that, everyone had built their own little den in the woodlands that surrounded the cove.

A few also had houses and cover businesses in town. Brody had chosen to build his home on the outskirts of town, closer than most of the outliers. His job as sheriff of the newly incorporated town of Grizzly Cove, Washington, demanded his full attention. Now that humans were coming into town with more regularity, he needed to stay on his toes so his brothers and their secret would be safe.

The town square had a plethora of art galleries that were filled with all kinds of stuff the bears had thrown together. Most of it was garbage, as far as Brody was concerned, but there were a few standouts. Drew's figurines had always been nice, and they were bringing in big bucks, mostly by accident.

Drew had put the first triple-digit prices on them as a joke, probably also hoping nobody would buy them. Much to his surprise, the rich humans who had bought the carvings on their way through town hadn't even blinked at the high prices.

That set the tone. After seeing the kind of money Drew was bringing into their community, it became a point of pride among the bears to try to do better. Even Brody had gotten caught up in the competition, learning how to use his chainsaw to carve logs into—what else— bears. He liked the irony, and the humans seemed to like the bears. They didn't bring in the same prices as Drew's miniatures, but Brody was working on improving his technique and learning to carve other things besides his self portrait.

When he wasn't busy being sheriff, that is. Not that there was much crime in their small town, but Brody's unofficial job was to keep an eye on the humans. In particular, he was watching over a trio of new arrivals who had gotten permission to open a business. Though humans had passed through, none but this group of three sisters had been brave enough to go before the town council—made up of the Alpha and his top lieutenants—to seek permits to open a business here.

There had been long, high-level discussions about the newcomers' bid to open a bake shop. Over a case or two of beer, the town council had decided to expand their social experiment to include the occasional human female in the town, under strictly controlled conditions.

Those conditions included discreet surveillance by the sheriff and strict limitations on where the females in question could live. In town. That was the only option open to them. Luckily, the sisters didn't seem to mind.

And so, Nell Baker—with the suitably ironic surname—and her two younger sisters, opened the Grizzly Cove Bake Shop and lived in the tiny apartment above the small store. Business was booming, because bears liked sweet things and because Nell and her sisters were easy on the eyes.

Nell, Ashley and Tina were also some of the only females for miles, though they didn't seem aware of it, at first. Only after they had set up shop and fallen into the routine of daily life, a few months after moving in, did they seem to realize there weren't a lot of other women in the area.

Oh, a few female bears had answered the Alpha's open invitation to settle in the cove, but times were tough in the realms of magic and those whose lives were touched by it. Most shifters seemed to want to stay put where they were until things settled down. Apparently, John hadn't really thought about that when he put his plan in motion, but it couldn't be helped now.

The shifter world was still in a holding pattern and would be until the enemy started up their old tricks again. Until that time, the bears were going to live…and live well.

"Afternoon, Nell," Brody said, walking into the bakery and finding the eldest of the Baker sisters manning the shop.

Brody liked to come by a few times a

week to check on things and pick up a pie. Nell made the most delicious strawberry rhubarb pies Brody had ever tasted.

"Now how did you know I just finished a batch of pies, Sheriff?" Nell laughed as she teased him.

Brody tapped his nose. "It smelled like lunchtime."

Nell rolled her eyes at him. "Pie isn't lunch, Sheriff." She motioned him to take a seat and brought over a cup of black coffee.

Because there weren't a lot of businesses in town where a person could get a meal, the bake shop had started serving coffee and sandwiches. The sisters baked artisanal breads in addition to the sweet stuff.

There were a few small tables inside, as well as a few wooden patio-style tables with umbrellas out front along the wide sidewalk. A lot of the men who found themselves in town during the day got their lunch from the sisters, and the ladies did a brisk business. The few tourists and hikers who came through loved the bakery too.

In fact, one walked in as Nell set Brody's usual turkey on whole grain sandwich down in front of him. She'd serve him the pie later, but she insisted he eat a proper lunch first, before he devoured the strawberry-honey-rhubarb confection.

Brody watched the tourist covertly as he ate his sandwich. There was something off about the guy, but Brody couldn't catch much of his scent from across the room and with the air conditioning unit blasting in his face. All he caught was the pungent scent of eucalyptus.

Maybe the guy had a sore throat and was sucking on a cough drop. Brody shrugged as he downed his sandwich, continuing to watch the tourist, his instincts telling him there was more wrong with the guy than just a summer cold.

Then the newcomer started speaking in a heavily accented voice, and his words told Brody all he needed to know. The man definitely had a one-way ticket on the bus to Crazytown.

"I heard there's supposed to be a lot of bears around here," the stranger said in a voice that carried to Brody, even as he stood to intervene. "But so far, all I've seen is a whole lot o' nothin'." The man leaned over the counter that separated them and took a very obvious sniff around Nell. Brody felt the growl reverberating in his throat as the man turned. "Finally!" he said, looking with challenge at Brody as he prowled across the floor of the bakery.

"You'd better leave the lady alone, son," Brody growled, moving closer.

"Why? I thought Grizzly Cove was the place where bears could be bears. Or is that just a PR slogan?" The man—scratch that, the *shifter*—was breaking all sorts of rules, including the most important. Don't let the humans find out.

"Let's take this outside, friend." Brody tried to intimidate the man out of the place, but apparently, a dominance contest was about to take place, whether he wanted it or not, and Nell was going to witness it. Goddess help them all.

He tried one more time, pitching his voice so only the newcomer would hear his words. "She's human, man. Don't be a fool."

"A fool! Who's calling Seamus O'Leary a fool?" the stranger demanded, reaching up to unbutton his shirt.

Only then, did Brody catch the underlying scent of alcohol.

"You're drunk," Brody snapped out, hoping Nell would accept that excuse for the man's bizarre behavior.

"I am not," Seamus objected, continuing to unbutton his shirt.

If the moron was going to get naked right here in the bakery and shift, Brody was going to have to do the same and show him who the bigger bear was in the most graphic terms. But Nell didn't know about shifters. And Brody didn't want to be the one to break it to her.

Better to arrest the drunken Aussie and handle all of this down at the station. When the foreign shifter sobered up a bit, then maybe Brody could make some sense out of his bizarre appearance.

Brody put one hand on the foreigner's shoulder. "Don't do this here," Brody coaxed. "Come with me, and we can do it properly."

Seamus shook his head. "Don't want to meet me in public, eh, mate? Why? What are you? A pansy-assed panda?"

Brody personally knew at least one resident of the cove who would take marked exception to that comment, but he was more worried about Nell, at the moment. The Aussie's shirt was off, and he just unbuttoned and unzipped, kicking off his sandals.

And then, he shifted. And got a lot smaller.

He wasn't a big man to begin with. Built more on the wiry side than the massive scale of most of the residents of Grizzly Cove. And he was gray. With tufted ears. And he wasn't chewing cough drops.

He was a fucking koala bear.

CHAPTER TWO

Brody learned, at that point, that koala bears—cute as they seem—have big fucking teeth. The furry little gray monster swiped at him with sharp claws and bared his chompers menacingly. The little bastard wanted to fight?

Brody looked at Nell's pale face. She was in shock, and Brody knew there was no putting this genie back in the bottle. *Shit.*

The crazed koala came after him again, and Brody had had enough. He tugged his embroidered golf shirt over his head and dropped trou, shifting seamlessly into his beast.

As a five-hundred-pound grizzly bear facing a comparatively tiny koala, the match was completely uneven. The koala seemed to realize it about the same time the alcohol he'd consumed when in human form caught up with him. He shuddered once, then collapsed into what Brody belatedly understood was a drunken stupor. The dude just passed out, right there on the bakery floor.

Brody sat back on his haunches, contemplating the hugeness of the mess the Australian had just created. Nell hadn't quite fainted, but she was visibly shaken. Brody didn't know how he was going to fix this.

And then, the Alpha walked in.

Big John took one look at the koala bear passed out on the linoleum and started to laugh.

Brody snagged his pants in his teeth and ducked behind a display case to shift. He struggled into them while the Alpha chuckled. When he emerged, dressed only in his uniform trousers, he looked at Nell but knew he had to square things with his Alpha first. It would be up to John, what happened next.

Although, if John had any thought about running Nell and her sisters out of town or trying to silence them permanently, he was going to have to go through Brody. He would protect the brown-eyed baker with every fiber of his being.

Whoa. That sounded serious.

Brody realized, in that moment, that all of the lunch hours spent here in the bakery were merely excuses to be close to Nell. He'd made up errands near the bakery, just so he could catch a glimpse of her through the window. And he'd come in more often than he probably should have.

All because of her. Nell. The sweet lady who baked the sweet pies he liked so much.

But he liked her even more.

Probably more than was good for him.

"I'm sorry, John. This guy just came in here and shifted before I could stop him," Brody said to his Alpha, leaving the more troubling thoughts about the pretty baker for later.

"I saw most of it, though I couldn't believe my eyes when he turned into a koala. Never seen a koala shifter in my entire life. Cute little fuckers, aren't they?" John bent down to get a closer look at the snoring marsupial. At that point, he seemed to get a good whiff of the stranger and backed off quick, shielding his nose. "Whew! Eucalyptus and alcohol. Not sure which one is stronger. I'm amazed he was sober enough to walk in here."

"He passed out. I can put him in a cell to sleep it off. Then, he's going to have to answer for his actions." Brody frowned. "And one of us is going to have to deal with the fallout." He glanced significantly at Nell, still standing with her mouth open, behind the counter.

John looked at her too, then frowned. "She saw you shift. You'd better talk her down. I'll take sleeping beauty to the jail." He held out his hand for the keys. "You give me a call if you need help with Nell."

John threw the small bear over one shoulder while Brody bundled the man's clothing into a ball that John tucked under one arm. Without a backward look, the Alpha was out the door and down the street a moment later.

Brody realized he was still shirtless, so he found his golf shirt and spent a few stalling seconds turning it right-side out. He pulled it over his head before turning to Nell, once again. She still hadn't moved.

"Are you okay?" Brody asked quietly, not wanting to startle her.

Nell blinked at him. "Was that…" She

18

paused, then tried again. "Was that real?" She gestured widely to the floor of the bakery and back to Brody. "You were a bear."

Knowing the time for lies was over, he nodded. "Yes, I am."

That got her full attention. She stared hard at him.

"You can turn into a bear?" Shock. She was definitely in some form of shock. "How is that possible?"

Brody shrugged. "I was born this way. It's what I am."

Nell just shook her head, clearly unable to deal with the revelation. Brody sighed.

"Look Nell, I'm the same guy you see every day. Now you just know a little secret about me." He tried to be casual. "And it *is* a secret. You understand? You can't tell anyone about us. The world isn't ready to know about shapeshifters."

"There are more?" She looked slightly appalled by the idea.

Brody wasn't certain if that boded well for getting her cooperation on this matter. And without her cooperation… He feared what the group might decide if Nell couldn't be counted on to keep their secret.

"Honey, this entire town is made up of shapeshifters. That's why it was so difficult for you and your sisters to get permission to open your store here. We weren't sure about letting humans in."

"Humans?" she repeated as if it was just sinking in, despite what she had seen. "You mean everybody is a...a...bear?" She looked outside at the people walking down the street, fear in her eyes. "Don't bears eat people?" she whispered, working up to a full-fledged freak out, if Brody was any judge.

He decided to tease her. Now that she knew the secret, she was fair game. And he'd seen her first.

"Only if they ask very nicely," he said in a husky drawl that made her gaze shoot back to his.

"Are you *flirting* with me? Now?" Outrage wasn't quite what he'd been aiming for, but it was better than panic.

At that moment, the little bell on the door jingled, and two of the town's most recent arrivals entered. Lyn Ling and her daughter, Daisy, had moved in last month. They were Chinese by birth, but the loss of her mate had sent Lyn running from her homeland, looking for a safe place to heal and raise her baby. Daisy was about four years old and cute as a button. She had just about every man in the settlement wrapped around her little finger, Brody included.

Daisy skipped up to the counter, looking with wide eyes into the glass display case as her mother said hello to Brody and Nell. As Nell looked from Brody to Lyn and back again, her eyes widened.

"You said everyone," Nell repeated. "Oh, God. Lyn too? And Daisy? They're...bears?"

Lyn scowled, looking at Brody. "What have you been telling her?"

"I didn't tell her. Some dumb drunk koala came in here and challenged my dominance right here in the middle of the bakery. Nell couldn't help but see. John left me to deal with it."

Lyn huffed at him. "Well, it's clear you're not dealing well." She then lapsed into Chinese muttering, probably saying unkind things about men in general, and Brody in particular, as she lifted her daughter into her arms. Pasting a smile on her face, she turned to Nell. "Yes, we are bears," she said firmly. "No, we do not hurt people. Not unless they hurt us first. We just want to live in peace. In harmony with nature. Free to be who we are. Is that too much to ask?"

Nell was left gaping at the outburst from the normally quiet woman. Slowly, Nell seemed to calm down. Eventually, she nodded.

"No, Lyn. It's not too much to ask. I guess, when you put it that way, it's kind of what everybody wants. Freedom to do what we wanted is why me and my sisters came here too. As long as you guys…bears…are okay with that, I think we can get used to the idea of people turning into grizzly bears."

"Not grizzly," Daisy decided to interject in her high voice. "Panda!"

CHAPTER THREE

"Oh, dear Lord," Nell whispered, completely overwhelmed by the craziness that had invaded her bakery today.

Maybe she was hallucinating. Maybe somebody had spiked the flour with PCP or something. That would explain why she was seeing koalas and grizzly bears in her store, and the cutest little four year old on the planet just claimed she was a panda.

"She better sit down," Lyn said in that no-nonsense way she had of talking.

"Yeah, I think you're right," the sheriff agreed, taking Nell's arm across the counter and guiding her out from behind. He escorted her to the nearest chair, and she let him.

She sat, only then realizing she was trembling from head to toe.

"You gonna faint on me, honey?" Brody

asked, squatting down in front of her chair.

He had that boyish smile on his face that usually made her knees weak. But they were already weak. They'd turned to rubber when the men had turned into bears, and only her death grip on the display case had kept her upright.

Nell had had a thing for the sexy sheriff since she first moved into her new shop. He'd come by to welcome her to town and had been by most days since, usually eating lunch here, while she covered the store. Her sister, Ashley, got up with the roosters and stayed until after the breakfast rush. Then, Nell took the afternoons, and little sister Tina covered the evening shift, which wasn't nearly as busy.

Nell was the oldest. She had brought her sisters here. Were they safe? Had she moved them all to an even more dangerous place than the one they'd just left?

Oh, God. Bending over, she wrapped her hands around her middle, feeling ill.

Brody's warm hand settled on her back, rubbing slow, pacifying circles as he moved closer. She felt surrounded by his warmth, but oddly, it made her feel safe.

This was the closest she'd ever been to

him. The barrier that had seemed to keep him at a distance was gone. But was her safety gone with it? Nell frowned, worrying.

"It's okay," Brody whispered. "You've had a shock. But you're safe, Nell. Nobody in town would ever hurt you."

A clatter on the table beside her made her look up. Lyn had brought her a strong cup of coffee.

"Drink up," Lyn said. "You need a jolt of caffeine. Only wish I had something stronger to give you." Lyn's smile was friendly, and Nell realized that the woman she'd become friends with over the past weeks was still the same, even if there was some bizarre way she could turn into a enormous bear.

Brody took the mug and handed it to Nell. He was such a gentle giant of a man. She had admired him from afar over the past weeks, glad his habit was to take a late lunch when the shop was quiet, as it was now.

Nell drank a sip of the coffee, and it did make her feel a little better. The heat of the liquid and familiar flavor of the brew grounded her a bit. It wore down the shock that had been riding her for the past fifteen minutes.

"Can you call Tina in to take over a little

early?" Brody suggested as she downed the coffee. "Tell her you're not feeling well or something?"

Nell's eyes widened. "Are my sisters safe here?"

Brody nodded solemnly. "Safer in this town than anywhere else," he insisted. "Our residents have all been vetted, and most have known each other for many years. While it's true we recently opened up to new faces, there's a procedure for shifters who want to join the community. That drunken Aussie wasn't supposed to just show up in town and go furry. He's going to face the Alpha when he sobers up, and believe me, that won't be pretty."

"We don't go around advertising what we can do," Lyn said, picking up her daughter once more. "Secrecy is the first rule of our society. You are now one of very few humans who know about us," Lyn went on. "Can you be trusted to keep our secret?"

Nell was surprised by the question. "I won't tell anybody," she promised. "Nobody would believe me anyway. I'd end up in the loony bin." She finished her coffee and put the mug back on the table at her side. Then she realized Lyn had come in to pick up the lunch order she'd called in an hour before. "Oh, you probably need to go. Let me get your bag," Nell said, rising and going behind the counter.

The familiar work helped calm her further, even if her world had been turned upside down in the past half hour. The lunch order was ready and sitting in the cooler. Nell took it out and handed it over the top of the display case to Lyn.

"It's on the house today, Lyn," she said when the other woman reached into her bag. "And there's a treat inside for Daisy."

The little girl's face lit up when she heard that last part. Her mother asked the universal mommy question. "What do we say when someone gives us a treat?"

Daisy responded with a loud, "Thank you!"

Nell couldn't help but smile at the child. "You're very welcome, Miss Daisy."

"I wouldn't leave, but I have a buyer coming to the gallery in twenty minutes. Promise me you'll come by later so we can talk?" Lyn insisted.

"I'll take good care of her," the sheriff insisted. Lyn shot him a doubtful look but left with a nod.

When Lyn had left, Nell found herself staring at Brody. His quirked eyebrow invited her to speak.

"So far today, I've seen a koala, a grizzly and, if Daisy is to be believed, a panda walk into my shop. In human form." As observations went, it was a doozy.

"I told John he should be more specific when he sent out the call for bears." Brody shook his head with a smile. "I was willing to bend the definition for Lyn and Daisy, but that puny Aussie? I don't think so. Besides, he smells like cough drops."

Nell laughed out loud but quickly stopped herself. "Eucalyptus. I think that's what koalas eat." She ran her hand through her hair in frustration. "God. I can't believe I'm even having this conversation."

"Actually, I'm kind of glad we're talking about it," Brody admitted, moving nearer, his arms crossed and his stance contemplative. "I've been wanting to get closer to you for weeks, but until you knew my secret, I had to keep my distance. I don't like lying to people I respect."

That took her by surprise. "You respect me?"

She couldn't imagine why. She was

nobody special. She was just another rolling stone who happened to land right side up in the cove, looking for a new start.

"Of course I do," he answered without hesitation. "You care for your sisters. You were strong enough to stand up for yourself, and for them, in front of the town council. You convinced Big John that you could make a go of your business here, and you've done just that. What's not to respect?"

When he put it that way... It was kind of charming of him to have noticed, actually. Nell felt her cheeks heat as she blushed. She'd been covertly watching the big sheriff every day since they'd met. He pushed all her buttons on a physical level, but also on a mental one. Their lunch conversations had ranged from the latest tech innovations in the news to the planning and layout of the town. She'd known he had a hand in it and liked what he had to say about the way he'd designed certain security aspects right into the road system itself.

"I respect you too," she admitted. "I like talking with you when you come in for lunch."

Brody sighed heavily. "But you're not sure what to make of the idea that I can turn into a grizzly at will, huh?" He gazed straight into her eyes.

She shrugged in reply. "I don't know what to think."

Rather than answer her, Brody reached for his cell phone and placed a call. Still feeling a little bewildered, Nell watched him as the call connected.

"Yeah, hi, Tina? This is Sheriff Chambers. I'm over at the bakery. Everything's okay, but I think your sister could use a bit of a break. She just finished dealing with a difficult customer. Is it possible for you to come in a little early?" He paused, listening to her sister's reply. "Excellent. We'll wait for you to get here." Another pause. "Yeah, I'm taking her out to decompress. I think she needs a little TLC after the day she's had. We'll probably just take a quiet walk around the cove." He smiled as her sister said something else. "Thanks. Yeah. We'll see you in a few minutes."

He ended the call with a tap of his finger and put the phone away. That little grin never left his face. He looked a bit smug. Was he feeling satisfied that he'd arranged to take her out? And how did she feel about his highhandedness? She honestly wasn't sure.

"You seem very pleased with yourself," she observed.

"That's because I am." His smile grew wider as he came around the display case, joining her in the work area as if he belonged there.

He took one of the empty boxes off the stack she kept ready and placed a few of the honey buns she knew were his favorites into it. She watched, bemused, as he put the box into a shopping bag and then pulled a few bills out of his pocket and stuck them in the cash register.

"What's that for?" she couldn't help asking.

"Our picnic," he answered, still grinning.

"What picnic?"

"The one we're going to take down by the beach while I tell you all about the bears and this town." He took her hand and led her out from behind the display case, even going so far as to remove her apron and fold it neatly before placing it on the counter. "Now that I'm free to speak the truth, there's a lot I want to tell you."

"What about my sisters? Will they be let in on the secret?" she wanted to know.

Brody's smile dimmed as he tilted his head. "I'm not sure. That sort of all depends."

"On what?" She put her hands on her hips as she faced him.

"On a few different things. How you handle what I'm going to tell you. How we proceed from here on out. What the Alpha decides. Any number of things, including your sisters' temperaments." He shrugged. "If it were up to me, I'd probably tell them, but when we agreed to settle here, we also agreed to follow Big John's laws. He's the Alpha. He gets to decide the big questions, like this one. But I wouldn't worry. He was the one who approved of your plans to open this bakery. He checked you all out before he ever agreed to let you into our town."

"He investigated us?" Nell was a bit insulted by the idea, but then again, it looked like these people—if that's what they were— had a lot to lose if they let the wrong sort of person run around loose in their community.

"Don't feel bad. He had us all investigated before he ever made the offer to let us live on his land. You probably don't realize it, but this place was Big John's dream from the get go. He quietly accumulated acres and acres of land around the cove over the past several decades. He plans long-term. And he wasn't about to let just anyone settle here."

"I had no idea. My rent goes to a big corporation, I thought."

"Yeah. A big corporation ultimately owned by John Marshall. He's got all kinds of paperwork and shell corporations that hide the fact of his ownership pretty well. That's why the lawyer was one of the first shifters he invited to join him here."

"The town lawyer is a...a shifter?" She tried out the unfamiliar term.

"Honey, everybody who lives here, except you and your sisters, are shifters. If you want to stay here, you're going to have to get used to it." He shook his head, his smile still charming, though his words were alarming.

"What if I want to leave? Would you let me go, now that I've seen what I've seen?"

Brody sighed. "That's another thing that would be up to the Alpha, though I would definitely argue in your favor. I don't think you're about to go hunting up the nearest newspaper reporter. And you also had no option when that crazy, drunk Australian forced the issue. It's not like you were deliberately trying to find out about us. You shouldn't have to pay the price for his stupidity."

"What kind of price are we talking about?" She had a bad feeling about this.

Brody started to look uncomfortable. "Well, in the past, some Alphas were known to impose permanent solutions for this kind of thing, but I don't believe Big John would even consider something like that in your case."

"When you say *permanent solutions*, do you mean…?" She couldn't bring herself to say it.

"Death," he said succinctly, nodding as she felt herself go faint. "I won't lie to you, Nell. Not anymore. Not even by omission. That's a promise." He held her gaze, and she felt some of his strength flowing into her, odd as it seemed. "But if it comes to that, I won't let it happen. I'll protect you with my own life, if I have to."

She believed him. She didn't know why, but she did.

"Let's hope it doesn't come to that, but thank you for the sentiment."

Brody moved closer, his hips in line with hers as his hands went to her waist. "It's not

34

a casual declaration, honey. There's something between us. I've felt it from the first moment I saw you. In a way, I should be thankful to that stupid koala, because now, I'm finally free to talk to you about who, and what, I really am."

CHAPTER FOUR

Tina showed up, and Brody stepped back, but not before her little sister got an eyeful of Brody Chambers standing right up in Nell's personal space. The big wink Tina sent her was almost comical. Nell would have laughed if the situation wasn't so serious.

As it was, she allowed Brody to hustle her out of the bakery in record time, Tina taking over during the slow mid-afternoon period. Nell usually used that time to do paperwork, but not today. Nope. Today, apparently, she was going to learn all about *shifter* bears.

She wasn't sure she wanted to know, but then again, spending time with hunky Brody Chambers was something she'd let herself think about off and on since moving to Grizzly Cove. She didn't think anything would ever come of it, but she'd let herself dream...occasionally.

Now she was getting her wish, but she honestly didn't know if she could handle the *why* of it. Suddenly, Brody was asking her out, but it wasn't for any of the normal reasons she had imagined. No, it was to explain the freakish nature of the town, and only after she knew all about it would the decision be made—by the Alpha, whatever that meant—as to whether or not she would be killed.

Hysteria tried to bubble up, but Brody took her hand and led her across the street toward the public beach area. It wasn't large, but the town—which was owned and operated by John Marshall, she had just learned—had put a few wooden picnic tables along the side of the road for public use. Beyond the sandy area, down a sloping incline, the waters of the cove lapped at the shore in a hypnotic rhythm.

Nell liked to go down to the water a few times a week to just listen for a bit and commune with nature. The town was out of the way and didn't see many travelers passing through, but that was okay by her. The residents bought enough of her breads and pastries to keep the bakery afloat, and that's all that really mattered. Nell wasn't here to make a killing. She'd come here to start over, with her sisters, and that was just what they'd done.

Now the only question was, would they be allowed to continue?

Brody let Nell sit before he placed the box with the honey buns on the table and sat opposite her. He didn't like the fear and uncertainty in her pretty eyes, but he understood why she was afraid. The unknown was usually frightening.

He hoped he could set her mind at ease, but he'd never done this before. As long as he'd lived, he had never had to explain what he was to anyone. They either had no clue, or they knew all about shifters because they were shifters too. Brody didn't usually hang out with humans.

But he found himself doing all sorts of new things when it came to Nell. From the first, she had stirred something in his blood. She had almost called out to him on some primitive level he didn't quite understand. Following his instincts, he'd spent time near her, having lunch at the bakery as often as possible, trying to figure out her allure.

So far, the only thing that had accomplished was to make her even more intriguing. And after today's debacle, he at least could be completely truthful with her at last. Only time would tell if that was a good thing or a bad thing.

He opened the box he'd packed earlier and bit into a honey bun before starting the conversation he knew he had to have with her. Honestly, he wasn't really sure how to do it, but he had to try.

"These are truly delicious," he said around a bite of the honey bun.

"Thank you. Ash makes them. I just do the glazing," she admitted.

"That's the best part," he said with a smile, licking his fingers absently. "Look, I'm not really good at this. I've never done it before. I've never had to tell anybody about shifters in my entire life, so I might mess up. Stop me at any time and ask questions, okay? Nothing is out of bounds now that you've seen my bear." He thought about his words. "Well...almost nothing is out of bounds. I'll let you know if we hit on a sensitive topic, okay?"

She smiled faintly and nodded. At least it looked like she was willing to try.

"Good. Now, the first thing you ought to know is that there are all kinds of shifters in the world, not just bears. Though we're among the most powerful, we're also far fewer in number than some of the others. There are tons of wolves, for example. A lot of big cats. Quite a few raptors. Get the picture?"

"You mean there are people that can turn into wolves and tigers and eagles?"

"Yep. But in Grizzly Cove, so far there are only bears. That's the way Big John designed this place. It was to be a haven for bears, specifically."

"Why?" she asked in a quiet but clearly interested tone. "Why only bears?"

"A number of reasons. Each of the original residents worked directly with John over the years. We're all bears, so we understood each other in ways we don't really understand the other shifters. Wolves have their Packs. Cats have their Clans. Bears...well...a lot of us are loners. We tend to stake out large territories and don't often interact with others of our own kind." He shrugged and finished the honey bun he'd been eating. There were still two left in the box.

"That sounds kind of lonely," she observed.

"It can be. But living too close to other bears can also be a problem. That's why most of us own property along either side of the cove. We need our space. The town is great for the times we want to be around other people, but the forest is home to the other half of our souls."

"That's kind of beautiful," Nell said quietly. He liked the soft, open, accepting look on her face. Maybe this was going to turn out okay after all.

*

They walked down to the waterline and then began a lazy stroll around the curve of the cove while Nell asked questions and Brody did his best to explain about shifters. He tried to gauge his progress by her mood. She was calmer now, which he took to be a good sign. And when her foot slipped on a wet rock, it was all the excuse he needed to put his arm around her shoulders.

There. That was better. He liked the feel of her petite frame under his arm. She was the perfect height for him. They *fit*, for lack of a better word. Just as he'd always suspected but had never been able to test out before.

It had been hell staying away from her. Not that he'd actually been able to stay *away*. He'd had lunch at her place more days than not, just to be around her. But he hadn't been able to touch her or ask her out. Or even walk on the beach with her.

That had all changed now, and Brody's bear side was pleased. As was his human side. Both wanted to get to know this lady much, much better, and they finally had the chance.

"You know, I'm glad you found out," Brody admitted after he'd explained as best he could and they'd turned their steps back toward the picnic area. They'd walked quite a way down the cove, away from the main street and toward the wilder areas bordered by dense woodlands. "I mean, the way you found out was kind of bad, but the result is something I can endorse, if it means you here with me, walking on the beach. I've wanted to ask you out for a long time, Nell."

"Then why didn't you?" She stopped walking and turned slightly to look at him. She was so close he wanted to bend down and kiss her.

"I couldn't. I didn't want to have to live a lie. I can't be only half what I am. I'm a man, but I'm a bear too. Both parts of me want to be near you." His words were impassioned, and he felt her respond, her small hands coming between them to rest against his chest as she moved even closer.

When her body swayed, he put his hand around her waist, his other arm still at her shoulders. He pulled her against him, and she didn't resist. In fact, she reached upward, standing on tiptoe. The invitation couldn't be any clearer, and he was happy to take it.

Brody lowered his head, and his lips met hers.

Sparks tingled through his body at the first touch of her lips. A sort of magic shimmered around him and through his bloodstream.

Nell didn't quite know how she'd ended up kissing Brody Chambers on a deserted stretch of beach, but she didn't mind at all. Not one bit.

There was something almost magical about his kiss. Something she'd never experienced before in a man's arms.

She felt…safe. Protected. Cared for.

And that was a lot of baggage to tack on to a first kiss, now wasn't it? But even though the undeniable fact that she'd seen him turn into a giant grizzly bear scared her on some level, the feel of his arms around her was something welcoming and warm. Like coming home.

Nell had always been a practical sort of woman. She knew she wasn't the prettiest of her sisters. That honor fell to the middle sister, Ashley. She probably wasn't the smartest either. Tina was the clever puss in her family. But Nell had grit. Determination to see that her sisters had as good a life as she could make for them all.

She'd always thought she had good judgment. But one kiss from Brody and all her best-laid plans of a long spinsterhood and non-involvement with the male of the species went right out the window. In his arms, she found she wanted this—for herself.

She had sacrificed a lot to keep her sisters with her after their parents died, and she'd always put them first. She had let her own desires take a backseat to making sure there was always food on the table and a safe home for her little tribe. But Brody made her want something for herself... Him.

She wanted him, and she couldn't deny the instant attraction she'd felt for him from the get-go. Now that she was finally experiencing his kiss, she could no longer blind herself to the fact that he was just about perfect in every way that mattered.

Oh, there was the bear thing. That had been seriously unexpected. She'd have to find a way to make peace with that in her mind...when Brody wasn't overwhelming her with his delicious kisses that tasted like honey.

CHAPTER FIVE

Brody walked Nell home a little while later, leaving her at the bakery door. She and her sisters lived in the small apartment above the store.

As sheriff of the sleepy town, Brody didn't have much to do normally. Today though, he had a drunk koala shifter in the tiny jail under his deputy's supervision that he had to deal with. Brody smiled as he walked down the main street, which ran along the apex of the cove. He'd finally been able to take Nell Baker in his arms and find out if her kisses were as sweet as the honey buns she baked.

He licked his lips remembering. Her kisses were even better than the buns, and that was saying something. He wanted more.

More importantly, his inner bear wanted more. It was the first time the grizzly inside

46

had sat up and taken notice of a female. Brody knew that meant something special. He had been wondering for weeks if the eldest Baker sister might not just be his mate.

But until the drunk shifter had shown up in her shop today, Brody hadn't been able to cross that final line. He hadn't wanted to get involved with her—with any female—unless she knew about his bear. He hadn't wanted to start something with Nell that could turn out to be serious with a lie of omission between them. Especially not something as big as he was when he shifted into bear form.

Now that it was finally out in the open and she'd seen his alternate shape, the self-imposed restriction was gone. He was free to court her and to talk about his dual nature. Oh, sure, the town council would probably meet and discuss the ramifications of letting the Baker sisters know about shifters, but Brody wasn't too worried about all that. Nell had heart. She would never betray him or any of the bears who called Grizzly Cove home.

Brody was whistling a jaunty tune as he entered his office. He had a koala to corral and a courtship to plan.

*

The next day dawned bright and clear. The Alpha stopped by the jail first thing and had strong words with their new guest.

As a result of Seamus's solemn promise to lay off the booze, straighten up and fly right, Big John had agreed to let him out. There was one condition. John demanded that Seamus make his way back to the bakery, with Brody as his police escort, and apologize to Nell for causing trouble.

And so, right before lunchtime, when Brody knew Nell would be manning the bakery by herself, but not too busy yet, he escorted Seamus into the store. Seamus, hung over and looking it, held his hat in his hands, his head down as he shuffled towards the counter.

Brody, by stark contrast, felt lighthearted at the vision of Nell, a little flour dusting the side of her cheek. She looked good enough to eat.

Down, boy.

"Morning, Sheriff," Nell greeted him.

"Miz Baker," he acknowledged with a

private smile just for her. When her cheeks flushed rosy under the sprinkling of flour, his smile grew even wider. "Seamus here has something he'd like to say to you. Miss Nell Baker, this is Mister Seamus O'Leary, originally from Australia."

The shorter man looked up sheepishly. "I'm sorry for the trouble I caused yesterday, ma'am." His voice had a decidedly Aussie twang to it.

Nell had met a few Aussies before and generally liked them. The overall impression she had was that they were hardworking people who knew how to party.

"My only excuse is that I just escaped from the private zoo of some corporate jackass with Gestapo security and cameras on me twenty-four-seven. I couldn't shift until I got free, and it was hard getting out of there as a koala. All they fed me was eucalyptus leaves, which are great normally, but the human side of me likes to have a little protein, now and again. And a few hops, preferably in beer form." He winked as his story lengthened and his manner became easier.

Brody stepped in. "When we founded the

town, Big John put out a call for any loners in the various bear shifter populations, hoping to attract females, honestly." Brody chuckled. "A few have applied for residency so far, and all, with the notable exception of Lyn and her child, are brown and black bears. Frankly, I've never seen a koala shifter before yesterday."

"We're rare," Seamus said, puffing out his chest.

Brody rolled his eyes before turning back to Nell.

"It's totally up to you, Ms. Baker, whether or not Seamus here is allowed inside your establishment. You can think over your answer and let me know later today." He didn't want to put her on the spot, and he liked the idea of knowing she would have to talk to him again that day, but she threw a monkey wrench into his master plan.

"No need. I can tell you right now that he's welcome, as long as he behaves. That means no drunkenness and no shifting inside, okay?" She looked straight at Seamus, and the other man had the sense to fidget under her no-nonsense scrutiny.

"I can promise you that, missus. Big John set me straight about the rules of this town, and I won't go breaking them again. I promise." The golden-skinned Aussie with the seriously Irish name seemed so contrite Brody almost believed him.

But Brody knew trouble when he saw it. And Seamus O'Leary had trouble written all over his furry gray koala ass.

"In that case, are you gentlemen here for lunch?" Nell asked, flashing a smile that hit Brody right between the eyes.

"Yes, ma'am," the koala answered without consulting Brody.

Not that he would argue. Any time spent near Nell was time well spent according to Brody. And if the Aussie was going to stick around in the bakery, better that Brody was here to keep an eye on him.

They placed their orders for sandwiches on the delicious artisanal bread Brody liked and sat at one of the indoor tables. He watched Nell bustle around behind the counter, liking the way her ponytail swayed as she worked.

Seamus nudged Brody's arm with his elbow. "You got something going on with the lady?" the koala shifter asked in a low voice.

Brody nodded once, staking his claim.

"Shame." The other man sat back in his chair. "You're a lucky man."

Brody nodded again, thinking truer words were never spoken.

Maybe Seamus wasn't so bad after all.

Nell came over a moment later with a large tray. It almost overflowed with the two plates holding substantial sandwiches, cutlery, napkins and condiments. Nell laid it all out before them, then pulled a small bottle out of her apron pocket and presented it shyly to Seamus.

"I wasn't sure…"

"Beauty!" Seamus exclaimed, taking the little jar from her. "I haven't had Vegemite in years. Thanks, doll. You're a peach."

Nell smiled, and Brody realized again how thoughtful this little human woman was. Here she was, facing the idiot who had revealed the existence of shifters to her just yesterday, in the most bizarre way, treating him to something special from his homeland. Brody could see the pleasure she took in providing Seamus with the small treat. It indicated how big her heart really was.

The koala shifter was right. Brody was the lucky one to have found a woman as extraordinary as Nell.

Brody and Seamus spent about an hour in the bakery, eating their sandwiches and finishing off with a slice of pie. Nell was kept busy as most of the people in town came in to pick up lunch. The town wasn't that big, but it seemed everyone who was in the area made it a point to stop by and talk to Nell.

A few of the women—and there weren't that many living here, yet—offered to answer questions Nell might have about their society. More than one gave Seamus the once-over. Apparently, news of the fracas here yesterday had gotten around. Brody was pleased to see the friendly overtures toward Nell. It seemed as if the bear shifter community was welcoming her.

It could easily have gone the other way. But maybe more than a few people had noticed them necking on the beach yesterday afternoon. Brody had been on the receiving end of a couple of envious looks and at least one high five. The latter coming from his deputy, earlier this morning.

Brody felt about ten feet tall, even in his human form. He liked that the others knew he was courting Nell. And he liked the subtle, silent approval from both his male contemporaries and the small, but growing, female population.

Before meeting John, Brody had always roamed alone. Now he was coming to appreciate the feeling of belonging, of being part of the larger bear shifter family.

When there was no longer any excuse to stay in the bakery, Brody parted ways with Seamus and made sure the Aussie shifter left the premises before Brody went up to the counter to speak with Nell. He didn't need an audience—especially not Seamus—for what he had in mind.

"Are you doing anything tonight?" Brody asked Nell as casually as he could, during a lull in business. The lunch rush was nearing its close, and the few people eating had chosen to sit outside.

"What did you have in mind?" Nell's smile was full of mischief and slightly shy. It was enchanting.

"I thought maybe I could make dinner for you. You've been feeding me for months now. I owe you a steak at the very least. You do eat steak, don't you?" For a moment, he had the horrific thought that she might be a vegetarian.

Nell chuckled. "I like steak. I can bring a

salad, if you like. We have some nice ripe lettuce plants on our roof balcony."

"You grow lettuce on your roof?" Brody couldn't picture it.

"There's lots of sun up there, and it's all just wasted space. We put a plastic patio table and chairs up there, and surrounded it with a container vegetable garden. Saves us a lot of money on groceries, and everything is super fresh."

"I had no idea," Brody said, charmed by the thought of a secret garden up on the roof.

"I'll show it to you, but not today. I know for a fact that Tina is sunbathing up there before her shift."

The way she said it made Brody think about Nell lying up there on a patio lounger. Naked.

He almost growled out loud at the image that popped into his mind.

"You should know, there are probably a few raptor shifters in the area. At least one eagle and a couple of owls and hawks. They don't usually have much to do with us, but occasionally, I see one fly over." He could see she wasn't quite making the connection. "If I can see them, they can most definitely see you up there sunbathing on your roof." Nell's mouth dropped open, and Brody had to grin. "It's something to consider." He shrugged. "You're not quite as alone up there as you might think."

Nell nodded. "Good to know." He could see the wheels turning in her mind.

"So. Dinner? My place?" he reminded her of the most important part of their conversation.

"Oh, yeah. I'd love to. What time?"

"How about I pick you up at seven when I get off shift?" Excitement flowed through his veins as both his human half and his bear half scented victory.

"Sounds perfect," she said, smiling at him with that shy look in her eyes that he found absolutely adorable.

He couldn't resist leaning across the counter and kissing her.

What he meant to be a quick peck turned into something molten as she kissed him back. Brody damned the counter that separated them, but thankfully, it kept him from going too far. The bell above her door jingled as somebody walked in on them, and Brody cursed inwardly.

Nell pulled back, her cheeks flushing a

lovely shade of pink while she looked toward the door and the newcomers who had interrupted them. She pasted a bright smile on her face and tried to pretend that they hadn't just been caught red-handed.

Brody whistled as he left, a spring in his step. He had a date, and if he played his cards right, he might just convince her to stay all night.

Or maybe forever.

CHAPTER SIX

Brody picked her up at the agreed time in his Sheriff's Department SUV. It wasn't very subtle, and everyone on Main Street saw him open the passenger door for her and help her in. They also saw the kiss he stole as he was assisting her up into the off-road vehicle, which had massive tires that made it a climb for her to reach the seat.

He chuckled at her momentary struggle, then solved the problem by lifting her around the waist and tucking her into the car. She squeaked, not expecting the move, but in the end, was grateful for the assist.

"I'm going to have to install running boards for you," he murmured. "But I like helping you in, too. Any excuse to touch you is a good thing as far as I'm concerned."

His words, coupled with the audacious wink he gave her as he closed the door, made her blood warm in her veins. He walked around the front of the large vehicle, and she noted he had no problem climbing into his own seat. The car was made for someone his size.

Suddenly, she felt small and feminine, which wasn't a sensation she often experienced. The oldest of the three Baker sisters, Nell hadn't had much time for dating after they lost their parents. She'd been eighteen and just barely able to hold her little family together. With the help of their elderly grandparents in those first few years, she'd been able to provide for the small family. When their grandparents died, too, the girls had been old enough to make their way in the world on their own.

Moving here had been part of the new start all three of them needed. They'd sold the home their grandparents had left them and unanimously decided to strike out on their own. After working for a successful bakery chain for years, all three of them knew the business and were able to take their skills with them.

Finding a place in the country had been ideal because of the lower cost of living. Their rent on the building wasn't much, and they had been able to squirrel away a bit of savings since opening the store, which they hadn't really expected.

Oh, they'd wanted to show a profit, of course, but hadn't projected any until next year at the earliest. But the people in Grizzly Cove had been amazingly receptive to the bakery, and business was booming. Well, as much as business could boom in a tiny town like this.

"How far is it?" she asked, to make conversation as they rolled past the last of the small businesses on Main Street.

"Not far. I live closer to town than most because of my job, but I managed to snag some property up on the hillside, with a lovely view of the cove. I think you'll like it."

Brody suddenly realized this was the first time he'd brought a woman to his new den. It was important to him that she liked the place. More important than it probably should be, but he found himself thinking in terms of forever where Nell was concerned.

If she liked the place, maybe she'd consider moving in with him? Maybe, if he could get even closer to her, he could discover if she was truly meant to be his mate. The bear inside him was still on the fence, but it was leaning more and more toward her each time they were near.

He'd deliberately held the bear back until yesterday because he couldn't have contemplated getting involved with her until she knew about shifters. Now that she knew, he had released his tight hold on his inner bear, and the cranky animal was being stubborn, withholding from the human side just for spite. Otherwise, he'd know already whether or not Nell was meant to be his.

Or so he believed. His parents always said they knew at first sight that they were meant for each other. In fact, Brody had spent an hour on the phone last night with his dad, trying to figure it out, but his dad had seemed to think that it was different for each shifter. Many, like his folks, knew immediately. Others had to be hit over the head with it.

Brody hoped he wasn't one of the latter. He wanted a mate. And a family. And a home that was more than just a house.

"I built into the side of the hill to take advantage of the views but did my best to leave the natural habitat intact," he told her. "Though there's plenty of room for a garden," he said, thinking of her rooftop oasis.

He looked over to find her smiling in a shy way that he found adorable. Pretty much everything about Nell was adorable. If he could pick a mate, he'd want a woman exactly like her. But one thing his dad had impressed on him in their talk last night was that shifters really didn't have much choice. True mates were granted by the Goddess and brought together by fate.

Brody pulled into the drive and drove up to the house, holding his breath to see her reaction.

"Oh, this is lovely," she exclaimed, and he started to breathe again. "I love the way the house blends into the woods. It's like it grew out of the hillside naturally."

Brody felt his cheeks heat as he flushed with pleasure at her compliment.

"It's my attempt at a human grizzly den. All the comforts and safety of being in the ground, and yet, the beautiful views and natural light my human side craves." He had never really put it into words before, but he found himself wanting her to understand.

She turned in her seat to look at him. "You really are two in one, aren't you? I mean, I've been thinking about it pretty much non-stop since yesterday, and I'm so curious about how it all works...being a bear, I mean."

He liked that she was interested. It was a good sign, as far as he was concerned. If she could accept his dual nature, maybe she would be amenable to being his mate. If the Goddess blessed them, of course. For now, the bear was withholding the knowledge from him, the furry bastard.

"Well, the first thing you need to know..." he said, pulling to a stop in front of the house and shutting off the engine, "...is that the bear side of me will never hurt you. I'm still me when I'm in my fur. I still know all my friends, and my protective instincts are in full force. You never need to fear the bear in me, Nell."

When she was silent, he turned to look at her and found her mouth open in shock again. Finally, she seemed to process his words. "I hadn't even thought about that. I mean, you were so great in the bakery yesterday, I guess I just didn't even consider it."

"Great?" She thought he'd been *great* in the bakery? He thought he'd scared her half to death, but apparently, she remembered it differently.

"Yeah, I mean, you could've torn up the place, or roared, or something. You could've wiped out that little koala with one swipe of your claws, but you showed enormous restraint, I thought. You were great," she repeated, nodding.

He was blushing again. He could feel the heat in his cheeks. He hadn't been so emotional since he was a teen, but something about Nell brought out all sorts of strange reactions in him.

"I probably should have sat on him at least," Brody joked, uncomfortable with the praise he didn't quite know how to handle.

Nell chuckled. "Then I would have had squashed koala in the middle of my shop." She giggled some more. "I shouldn't laugh. It's just a funny visual, you know? Like a cartoon or something."

"It would've been a little ridiculous," Brody admitted, smiling with her. "I just couldn't bring myself to hurt the little guy. I mean, he was stupid and drunk. And did I mention stupid? But there's something about a koala. They're not a real bear, you know? But they're kinda cute if you hold your breath."

"Why hold your breath? Oh! You mean the eucalyptus smell?" She chuckled again. "He kind of smelled like a cough drop to me."

"Well, I've heard that smell is intense for humans, but imagine how my nose reacted to that. We smell things, hear things, taste things…a lot more than you do. Our senses are way more acute. His scent is literally an assault on the nostrils."

"I had no idea, but I guess it makes sense. Wow. You continue to amaze me the more I learn about you," she said candidly.

He liked that she wasn't holding things back from him. He'd seen her shock and her fear, though thankfully not too much fear. Her honesty was fresh and welcome.

"Then let me amaze you even more with my grilling skills. I've got everything set. All I have to do is light the fire and get things cooking." He gestured toward the house. "Shall we?"

She smiled at him, and his heart stopped for a moment. "Sure. But I'm going to need some help getting out of your car, or I might fall on my nose."

"Say no more. Your wish is my

command."

He got out of the vehicle and walked quickly around to her side, opening the door and lifting her out.

He took his time lowering her to the ground, allowing her body to slide against his all the way down. And even when both of her feet were on the ground, he didn't let her go. He paused, letting her decide if she wanted to step away and break their connection.

When she didn't, he lowered his head and stole the kiss he'd been wanting since the night before. A kiss with no holds barred. Nobody watching. Nobody gossiping. Just the two of them, in the forest evening.

His arms swept around her when her knees crumpled, and he felt the sharp stab of pride knowing he'd nearly made her swoon with pleasure. Just from a kiss. He wondered what would happen when they finally made love. And then, he almost growled out loud, thinking about how much he wanted that to happen tonight.

He tightened his hold, wanting to feel every one of her luscious curves against his starving body. But then, he made himself release her, one agonizing inch at a time. He couldn't rush this. He had to remember she was human. She probably didn't feel the same raw urgency as shifters did. He had to do this right and give her all the space she needed.

Of course, that didn't mean he wasn't going to do his best to seduce her, but he'd lured her to his den with the promise of dinner. He could at least feed her before he tried to convince her to go farther. Besides, he liked spending time with her. Sex would be great—no, it would be awesome—but he also wanted to just have her in his space for a little while, all to himself, to enjoy talking with her and basking in the sparkle of her eyes.

CHAPTER SEVEN

Nell's head was spinning when Brody let her go. She was dazed and didn't really comprehend at first why he'd stepped back. She had been on the point of climbing his body like a tree and removing his clothing with her teeth. Even now, she had to fight the impulse to step closer and demand he give her more of those addictive kisses.

She wanted to run her fingers over his body, to learn the curves and hardness of his muscles. Brody was, by far, the finest specimen of a man she had ever gotten this close to. She hadn't been in town long before she noticed that he filled out his clothes with amazing detail, his shoulders straining at the seams of his embroidered uniform golf shirts.

She liked the casualness of this town's sheriff's uniform—those nice, stretchy golf shirts that showed off every muscle when he moved a certain way, and cargo pants that showcased a tight ass she had found herself watching every time he walked out of the bakery. Brody Chambers had a great butt.

And he was a truly nice guy too. Not vain, he didn't even seem to be really aware of how good looking he was. As she was getting to know him, she had figured out that he came by his muscles honestly, doing all sorts of physical labor around the town when needed. He wasn't the kind of man to sit on the sidelines when something needed doing, and she really admired that.

As her head began to clear, she realized he was looking into her eyes as if to gauge her reaction. She felt like a fool, caught staring at him, probably with a goofy expression on her face.

The man was lethal. His kisses should come with mandatory warning labels. *May cause dizziness, light-headedness, lack of oxygen to the brain and gooey, lovestruck appearance. Oh, yeah.*

"Ready to eat?" His voice rumbled through her body, warming her in very private, sensitive places.

You bet she was ready. But it didn't

sound like he was on the menu at the moment. Nell tucked away her disappointment and tried to sober up. He'd invited her here for dinner. She had to get with the program!

"Where did you put the bag I gave you?" she asked, buying time to settle her nerves.

Brody went to the backseat of the big SUV and removed the large shopping bag she had packed earlier and given him when he'd picked her up. He closed the car door and hefted the bag in one hand as he motioned for her to precede him up to the front door.

He reached around her to open the door and let her walk through first. The house was lovely. Although built into the side of the hill, there were lots of windows at the front and skylights in the front part of the roof that let the twilight of outside into the structure. It almost felt like a continuation of the woodlands she had just stepped out of. The house was rustic and majestic all at the same time.

Rough hewn beams and giant poles that had to have been entire tree trunks dominated the entryway but gave way to more modern materials at the back where the house entered the hillside. There was a techno-forest vibe where the wood blended with poured concrete slabs and brick that had been artfully arranged as walls and supporting structure. The house was definitely built to last.

"You built this yourself?" she asked, not quite believing it. This house should be on the cover of a design magazine.

"Every beam and every brick," Brody said, and she heard the hint of pride in his voice. He should be proud. What she could see of it was amazing.

"Wow." She moved farther into the giant living room, which fronted the house, probably to take advantage of the awesome view.

"So you like it?" He seemed unsure.

"Like it?" She turned to meet his gaze. "Brody, this place is like nothing I could have imagined. It's ingenious. I love it."

Hearing her sincere approval of his efforts did something to Brody. It was like a great weight had been lifted off his shoulders, and a smile started inside his heart, working its way outward. She liked the den he had built for his mate.

Oh, he hadn't been consciously aware of it, at the time, but Brody had always had a little ray of hope, somewhere in the back of his mind, that he might find a mate to settle with after he put down roots in Grizzly Cove. He'd designed the house on a much larger scale than he'd need just for himself. He'd also put in every modern convenience a woman—or a growing family—could need. And safety had never been far from his mind. The entire back half of the house could be sealed off like a fortress if attack came from the open front half, and there was even a secret tunnel escape route if they got trapped in the underground section.

He'd tried to think of everything. He had put a lot of effort into both the design and the construction. This was his home, and he would hate to have to leave it, but he would, if his mate didn't approve.

Whoa. There was that word again. *Mate.*

Why was it that he kept thinking about a permanent arrangement when it came to Nell? She was human, which would make life difficult, but she was also so…incredibly perfect. Maybe the shifter mate he'd always envisioned in his life wasn't meant to be. Maybe he was meant to have a human mate.

Oddly, the thought didn't bother him as much as he expected it would. Not when the human woman in question was Nell.

For her, he'd do just about anything. She was delicate, so he'd have to temper his more animalistic tendencies, but his bear was starting to think of her in *mate* terms too, so it wanted to protect her. If the bear decided she was it, then the human half of his nature wouldn't argue. His human side had been attracted to her from the very beginning. It was the bear that had reserved judgment.

And now, the bear was puffing out Brody's chest, proud that the small woman liked the den he had built.

"Come on back to the kitchen. We'll just get the grill started, and I'll put the steaks on," he said, focusing on the task at hand.

He'd invited her over for dinner. He would make sure he actually served the food before he lost complete control and pounced on her. It was the least he could do.

The kitchen was in the front part of the house that stuck out from the hillside. It was off to the left side and had a door that led to an outdoor deck that was secluded by pine trees and the surrounding forest. There was a wooden table and chairs out there Brody had carved from tree trunks and stained to match the environment. He'd spent many evenings out on this deck, from which he could see the front of his property through the screen of branches but remain hidden from view.

"It's like a hidden grotto out here," Nell observed as he led her outside.

He'd left her shopping bag on the kitchen island before heading out to light the grill. If he didn't get the fire going, it would be a long wait for those steaks he'd promised her.

"I eat out here most of the time," Brody admitted, rolling back the wooden cover he'd made to camouflage the huge grill that was his pride and joy.

"Wow," Nell said, peering at the propane-powered giant that filled the back of the deck. "That's some grill."

Brody beamed. "One of my little indulgences," he admitted. "Bears like meat, and my human side likes it cooked to perfection. This grill is the compromise, so I went all out to get the best one I could afford when I built this place. I cook out here almost every night."

"What about when it rains?" This part of the country received a lot of rain, but he'd come up with a way around that too.

"Behold," he said, like a showman, as he pressed a button and the canopy he had painstakingly designed deployed to cover the deck.

"That is so cool," Nell whispered as she looked up to admire the dark green canopy he had rigged so that any rain would slide off to either side, away from the house. It kept the deck and grill area dry while not cutting them off from the night air or the view. She turned back to look at him. "You've really thought of everything. I'm impressed."

Brody couldn't resist. He leaned down to steal a kiss.

The taste of her mouth was like ambrosia to a starving man. Honey and light. Sweetness and life.

Brody lifted her in his arms and seated her on the wooden table, moving between her thighs. The feel of her soft body flowing around him made him tremble. How much better would it be when they were skin to skin and he could sink inside her tight warmth, learning the feel of her body taking him…accepting him?

He wanted that with every fiber of his being. He wanted to belong to her and have her belong to him. The human side was totally on board with that concept, but the bear was still reserving judgment, though he was starting to see the merits of having a soft human woman share his den. She would bring laughter and wonder...and cubs.

Even if she could never run with him in the woods and hunt by his side in bear form, he would have cubs to teach and play with. Young to raise and love. His mate would love them, and he would love her. They would make a family. The bear approved of that idea wholeheartedly.

"Brody." His name was a whispered plea on her lips, driving his passions higher.

He lowered his lips to her throat, nipping a little, enjoying her flutters and the small squeak when he pushed a bit too hard. He drew back, meeting her gaze.

"I'm sorry. We should eat first." He stepped away, though it was one of the hardest things he had ever had to do.

"First?"

He had turned away but looked back at her to gauge her reaction. Her tone had been flirty. The look on her face was...daring. She was smiling, and one eyebrow was raised in question.

"Uh..." He cleared his throat. "I

mean…"

Nell hopped off the table and walked slowly over to him, placing her right hand over his racing heart. She was still smiling, and he wasn't entirely sure he knew what to make of her expression. She looked…confident, as if she knew something he didn't. Hell, she probably did. Women were mysterious creatures, and Nell was a prime example of her species.

"It's okay, Sheriff, I know what you mean." She tapped her fingers over his heart playfully, and his breathing hitched. "As it happens, I think we're thinking along the same lines." She stepped back when he would have given in to his instincts and reached for her. "I'd like my steak medium well," she said brightly, and it was some time before he could make his brain work again, and figure out that she had just placed her dinner order, as it were.

So much for thinking along the same lines, he thought sadly. But he had promised her dinner, and it looked like she was hungry, so he would feed her. And bask in her presence.

He liked having her in his home. She added a liveliness to the place that didn't normally exist.

"I'll just go get the steaks," he said, heading back into the kitchen after lighting the grill.

She followed on his heels, going straight for her shopping bag. The bag was full of plastic food boxes, which she unpacked neatly, and he realized as they worked in the kitchen together that she'd brought way more than just a fresh salad.

"What is all that?" he asked, unable to contain his curiosity.

"Just a few other things you can put on that massive grill to go with the steaks. It all came from our garden."

"Seriously?" His jaw practically dropped when she opened and unwrapped savory green and red peppers, sweet potatoes, zucchini, and what looked like a small gourd or squash of some kind. "That can all go on the grill?"

She smiled up at him. "Give me a little corner of that rack, and I'll show you what can be done with roasted veggies." The largest plastic bowl did, indeed, contain the promised salad. She'd also brought a bottle of homemade dressing. "I hope you like raspberry vinaigrette."

"Bears love berries," he answered, his stomach rumbling a bit in anticipation. Usually the bear inside him was placated by meat, but it craved sweet things too, which is why he often stopped in at the bakery for a slice of pie or a honey bun. "In fact, there's a wild patch a short way up the hill. I go there sometimes, when the berries are ripe," he found himself admitting.

He had never told anyone about his private berry patch and felt a little foolish for doing so. Rolling around in a berry patch in his fur was one of his sweetest memories of childhood. His mother would take him out in the forest behind their home and forage with him. Those were some of the best days he could remember as a child.

"You know, you could probably cultivate more berries up here." She looked around as they stepped back onto the deck. "Berries love this volcanic soil and climate. I bet I could get blueberries, blackberries, even raspberries to grow here."

He liked the sound of that. More than the berries, he liked the idea that she would even consider nurturing the land around his home and making things grow. She had a giving nature and both his human and bear side liked it. A lot.

They worked side by side at the grill for a while. She grilled her vegetables, teaching him a thing or two, while he took care of the steaks. Before long, they had full plates and, not long after that, full bellies. They'd eaten her salad, then followed that with the steaks and veggies. All in all, it was one of the most memorable meals Brody ever had in this house.

"How long have you lived here?" Nell asked as they lingered over the dessert she had also brought in her shopping bag of tricks.

"Not too long, really. About two and a half years," Brody admitted. "The town sort of sprang up overnight once Big John told us his plans. We all pitched in, and we got some help with the legal side from the shifter leaders. We call them the Lords. They have connections in every state and in the federal government."

"Bears in the government?" she asked with a teasing smile.

"Actually, they're werewolves, but it's the same concept."

"Werewolves?" she repeated the word incredulously. "Like in the old movies?"

"Not really. They turn into wolves, just like I turn into a bear. Technically, you could call me a werebear, or weregrizzly, but I like just plain ol' *shifter* better." He thought about the old movie creatures and tried to give her a more complete answer. "There is a battle form though, which is probably where those old movies got their start. It's the halfway point between human and wolf—or human and bear—that is a bit of both, and it's pretty effective for fighting, if you can hold it. Only the strongest of us can hold the shift in the middle for any length of time. As youngsters, we practice it, and it helps us figure out the hierarchy of strength and dominance."

"The whole concept is kind of fascinating," she said, making him glad he had tried to explain things for her. "And I'll admit, it's a little scary too."

He didn't like that.

"You don't ever have to be afraid of me, Nell. I would never hurt you, no matter what form I'm in. Even if my instincts are sharper as the bear, I'm still me. I still think and feel and know what I'm doing."

She paused, and he held his breath, but then, she met his eyes. "I'm not too worried about you, per se, Brody. It's the others. I don't know all of them, and I worry for my sisters. What if they say or do the wrong thing? A regular guy who wasn't very nice might get abusive, but what would happen if a guy who had the strength of a bear got angry?"

"I won't lie. We're stronger and more dangerous than the average human man. For one thing, we can sprout claws and sharp teeth, and we don't shy away from using them. But we're also somewhat better at curbing our baser instincts. Shifters have been living in secret among humans for centuries. Millennia, even. And for the most part, we've been able to fly under the radar. We couldn't have done that if we had poor impulse control." He wanted her to be sure about him and about the other bears in town. He didn't want her to be afraid. "And even before you moved in, Big John read everyone the riot act about how you and your sisters were to be treated. Bear society might not be as hierarchical as say, the wolves, but the Alpha's word is still a law. Until that silly koala rolled into town yesterday, you and your sisters were not to be told—or shown—the truth about us."

"But how could we have lived here for

any length of time without the truth coming out?" Nell wanted to know.

Brody sighed. "John had you vetted carefully. He seemed to think that, if you did find out, you weren't the kind of people who would go running to the tabloids. But the whole thing was supposed to be a test run, to see if we could let more humans into the neighborhood and live among them without anybody being the wiser."

Nell sat back in her chair, thinking. "Well, until yesterday, it was working. I had no idea."

"Yeah, I know." He had to smile. "It was killing me, you know? I wanted to be able to talk to you. To ask you out. But I didn't want to start anything unless you knew the full story about me. Yesterday sort of untied my hands, and in a way, I should be thankful to that damn troublesome Aussie."

Nell looked kind of…angelic, in that moment. The lighting on the deck was dim and yellow, to keep down the bugs. They were sitting on the same side of the table, closest to the grill. It didn't take much to lean forward in his chair and kiss her.

She didn't resist. In fact, she leaned closer to meet him. And then, the fire truly started.

He lifted her out of the chair and positioned her on the clear end of the large wooden table, taking his place between her thighs as he had before.

He kissed her deeply, enjoying the taste of her, the feel of her soft curves against him. He liked the way her hands moved over his body, almost petting, clenching when he did something she liked, the little rounded, human nails digging into his skin through the fabric of his shirt.

And then, her fingers were undoing the buttons of that shirt, and his breath caught. She seemed so eager. Was she ready for what he had in mind? Did she want him like he wanted her? Would she let him go all the way? Was she ready for the consequences?

What if she really was his mate?

CHAPTER EIGHT

The thought stilled him. Brody lifted his lips from hers and moved back a tiny bit so he could meet her eyes.

"I want you to know…" He paused to catch his breath. "There's a very real possibility that if we do this, I'll want to keep you."

The way her eyes lit up made his heart clench.

"What if I want to keep you too?" Nell countered after a moment's pause.

"Honey, if you're my mate, you won't be able to get rid of me." He needed to make her understand. "And that's the truth. Mating is for life among shifters. So if you're not sure about this…"

Goddess, he was going to kill himself later for being so noble. But if she really wasn't sure and wanted out… He had no choice. He had to let her go if she asked. His honor demanded no less.

"How will you know if I'm your mate?" she asked, her fingers running up and down his arms in a playful way that made him want to growl.

"Once we make love, my inner bear will either want to claim you or be indifferent. If the bear is indifferent, there's not much the human side can do about it." He had to be brutally honest with her. She deserved the truth.

"So it's all or nothing?" He didn't like the way her eyes shifted to the side. That she wouldn't meet his gaze told him something.

"It would never be nothing. Not between us." He stroked a strand of her hair back to tuck behind her ear. "I admire you. I think you're amazing in almost every way, Nell. I just want to be honest with you. I value the truth, and you deserve it. I wanted you to know that if, and when, the bear gets a taste of you and decides he likes it, there's no turning back. If the bear recognizes you as his mate, it's for life, so I wanted you to be forewarned."

"How likely is it?" she whispered shyly.

Brody stifled a growl at her unconsciously

sexy tone. "I think it's very likely."

"So mates means…what? Is that like, you'd want to marry me?" She sounded so hopefully unsure it was kind of a turn on.

"Mating is more than marriage. It's forever. It means everything a human marriage does and more. Like building a family together, if that's what fate has in store."

"Children?" She seemed happily surprised. "Would they be like you? Little bears?"

"Probably," he admitted. "Either way, they'd be loved." He sensed her approval of his words. "The thing is, mating is not something you can end with a legal document. When I say it's forever, I mean *forever*. I could never let you go, Nell." He cupped her cheek in his palm. "You would be mine, and I would be yours. For the rest of our lives."

"So…um…how does the bear know?" she asked, moving closer to him, almost breathing her words against his lips. "I mean, you'll be human when we…um…"

He thought he knew what she was driving at, so he helped the conversation along. "I will only make love to you in my human form, since you are human. Frankly, doing it as a bear has its limitations, so I won't miss it. Though it might be fun to play chase with you occasionally. The bear likes to hunt."

Her eyes widened, but he didn't let her talk anymore. The important things had been said, and she hadn't run from him. No, she had stuck by him through the awkward revelations. She had seemed more intrigued and hopeful than fearful. There was nothing more to say. Now was the time for action.

His words gave Nell pause, but not enough to want to stop. She'd never responded so completely to a man, never wanted a man so much. She felt in her heart that Brody was someone special to her, even if he was a being totally outside her previous experience.

The whole concept of shapeshifters still kind of blew her mind, but she'd known Brody for a while now, and in all that time, he'd always been a man she could admire, respect, and definitely want to get to know better. Now was her chance, and she was going to reach out and take it with both hands.

She was going to reach out and take him

with everything she had. The need building inside her would not be denied. And, somehow, she trusted that the future would take care of itself. If they were supposed to be together forever, it would happen.

She liked the idea a lot. Brody was the kind of man a woman could build a life with. He had all the qualities she admired in a man—and then some. The whole bear thing... Well...even though it was still a little scary, it was also kind of a turn on. All that leashed power was very attractive in an uncivilized, throwback sort of way. Nell hadn't realized she was so old fashioned, but something about Brody holding all that magic and strength inside him was incredibly attractive.

He wasn't hard on the eyes either. Muscles on muscles, Brody had the kind of physique women drooled over. In fact, she and her sisters had noticed how well most of the men in the area were built. It had been the topic of conversation between them, for weeks now. They'd put it up to the rustic setting, and the fact that most of these men worked hard at physical jobs and tasks around town and on their properties. Now Nell knew another facet—they were all shapeshifters who could turn into bears.

Her sisters would never believe her if she tried to tell them. Smiling inwardly at that thought, she didn't resist when Brody moved closer. And then, she didn't have any truly cohesive thoughts for a very long time as he showed her how a shapeshifting man could worship a female body.

More than that though, she felt like, of the few men she'd been with, Brody was the first one to think more of her comfort than his own. He undressed her as if she was made of some priceless, fragile substance. And when she pushed at his shoulders and fisted her hand in the fabric that still covered him, he took the hint and quickly removed the offending material.

His skin was hot and only slightly rough against her palms. For a guy who turned into a bear on a regular basis, he wasn't all that hairy. She loved the feel of his muscles moving under taut skin, and his big hands were as patient with her as she could have dreamed. He was a considerate lover, which was something she'd always looked for in a man. A gentle giant.

Exactly like Brody.

She gasped as he cupped her bare breasts,

his fingers rubbing her nipples. He teased her skin with deliberate touches that drove her passions higher. Each little lick of his tongue over hers, and his fingers over her breasts, made her want more.

His mouth moved downward, over her jaw, into the sensitive hollow of her neck and then, lower. His palms positioned her breasts for him to lick and suck. Little noises of pleasure issued from her throat without her conscious volition.

He lay her back on the table, coming down over her, blanketing her with his warmth. Her remaining clothes disappeared as if they had melted away, and her mind spun as he kissed a trail down over her abdomen and into the warm crevice between her thighs.

Never in her life had she felt such sensations. Brody played her body like a master, and she suddenly realized that any other sexual experiences she'd ever had could never compare to this moment...to this man. Brody was unique.

"Mmmm," he rumbled against her most sensitive spot, making her quiver. He paused and looked up at her, meeting her gaze from between her thighs. "Know something bears really like?" he asked rhetorically, pausing a beat as their gazes held. Then he smiled. "Honey."

Leading with his tongue, he renewed his gentle assault, driving her higher until she shattered. She came, and he rode her through it, gentling her and drawing out the climax.

When her body started warming up again—much to her surprise—he stood and removed his pants, the final barrier between them. The shape and size of him was impressive. She almost laughed, thinking of the way she and her sisters had been speculating about all the hunky guys in town. Based on what she was seeing here, her sisters would have to revise their estimates…up. Way up.

Brody was hung like a bear. The thought crossed her mind, and then she nearly dissolved in giggles. The only thing that saved her was that, at that very moment, Brody stepped closer once more, tugging her downward on the huge table until her splayed thighs were in the perfect position to receive him.

And then, all thoughts fled her mind once more as he joined them. Skin to skin. She would think about that later too, once her mind was out of the clouds and back on Earth. For now, though, everything was perfect. Brody was perfect. Big but perfect for her.

He touched places inside her body—and in her heart, as well—that no man had ever touched before. He filled her, claimed her, and made her his own.

Even if his bear didn't think she was his mate, Brody the man was going to have a hard time getting rid of Nell after this. Just let him try. She could be every bit as possessive as a grizzly bear.

Then he began to move.

Sweet mother in heaven, Nell wasn't sure she was going to survive. The pleasure built in slow waves as he began an advance and retreat, like water lapping at the shore. The gentle lapping turned into an ocean current as his motion increased and then into a torrent as they were both swept up in something beyond control.

The tempest was upon them, pushing her to the height of pleasure, demanding and giving all at the same time. She clung to Brody's shoulders. He was her one solid presence inside the raging storm. He was her anchor and her rock. He was the one who would protect her and push her beyond all boundaries. He was her lover and, if she had anything to say about it at all, her mate.

She screamed his name as the crashing wave broke, casting her higher than she had ever gone before. His muscles tightened as her body clenched around him, and together, they rode the gentler waves of completion, held secure in each other's arms.

CHAPTER NINE

Without saying a word, Brody carried her into the house and back to his bedroom. Something profound had just happened, but he'd be damned if he was going to tell her she was his mate while they were still wrapped up in a quickie on the picnic table. Even if it had been the most earth-shattering quickie of his life.

He lay her down in his bed, marveling for a moment at how good she looked there. Her body was luscious, curved in all the right places and a perfect fit for him in every way. Much as her personality and sharp mind seemed to mesh with his. She challenged him and fascinated him. Theirs would be a really good match, he'd thought from the first.

Now he knew his inner bear was on board. All he had to do was tell her...and hope she felt the same.

It was a tricky business, mating with a human. They didn't have the same instincts as a shifter. There was no inner furball telling her what must be.

Brody was taking a big chance here. He was fully committed—but could she be, without the inner beast driving her? He didn't know, but he'd sure like to spend the rest of his life finding out.

He settled in the bed next to her, his arm lying over her waist, his legs tangled with hers. He needed the skin contact even as their breathing started to return to normal.

He felt her move. He looked over to find her leaning up on one elbow, smiling at him.

"So, what's the verdict?"

Brody wanted to laugh. He should have known his Nell would take life by the balls and face whatever would come of their joining head on. He loved the way she didn't back down.

He levered himself over her, kissing her and aligning their bodies, reveling in the feel of her softness beneath him. If all went well, he'd feel these sensations for the rest of his life.

But he had to tell her and see what she'd say. He couldn't put it off any longer, even if he was just a tiny bit afraid of rejection. He had to be a man and face her. If she didn't want to be his mate, he'd just have to spend the rest of his life finding ways to convince her. He could do that, couldn't he?

Brody lifted his head, ending the kiss, and met her gaze.

"You're mine, Nell. My mate. Now and forevermore."

She gasped but didn't say anything while his heart climbed quietly into his throat. Why didn't she say something?

Finally, she took pity on him. Her smile gave him hope as she leaned closer to whisper against his lips.

"I like the sound of that. Because you know what? You're mine too. And I'm not ever letting you go."

She sealed her words with a kiss, nearly tackling him with her enthusiasm. She ended up on top this time, and he didn't mind a bit. She sank down onto his hardness and began a slow, perfect ride that sent his senses soaring.

He let her do with him what she willed. He was her slave. Her partner. And her protector. Now and forever.

As that crossed his mind, another thought

occurred, and he broke their kiss, taking her by the shoulders to still her movements.

"Does this mean you'll marry me?" He had to know she was willing to be his in the eyes of the human world, as well as by shifter standards.

"You're asking me this now?"

She was laughing, her face aglow with the dew of her exertions. He wanted to lick her all over. Her breath came in labored pants as she tried to squirm on him. She had been nearing a peak, and he'd stopped her as his thoughts overcame his instincts.

"I need to know," he said softly, hoping she would understand.

But she was his mate. Of course she understood. He saw the softening of her expression as she looked deep into his eyes. He had the sensation that she could see down all the way into his soul.

"Yes, Brody. I will marry you. It would be my honor to spend the rest of my life with you and make this house a home."

That's all he needed to hear. He kissed her, rolling with her so he was on top. He took over the work of grinding into her, driving her pleasure as high as he possibly could before he took his own. She came at least three times before he lost count and joined her in bliss.

He'd found his mate, and she was going to marry him. More than that, she liked his den enough to want to share it with him. Life couldn't get much better than that.

It was after they had both come back from the biggest climax yet and were laying side by side in the bed when she spoke again.

"We're going to have to tell my sisters, you know." She sounded both worried and amused.

He liked the little designs she was tracing over his arm with her finger, absently petting him in a way he knew he would love getting used to over the next several decades. He looked over at her to find her staring at the art he'd painted on his bedroom wall last winter. It was a mural of a grizzly being followed by two cubs. It had been a hopeful bit of whimsy on his part, a dream of what he hoped someday might be in his future. And now, with Nell in his life, he finally had a chance at a family, if the Goddess so blessed them.

"I'm trying to think how to tell them without scaring them," Nell went on, oblivious to his deeper thoughts. That was okay. There was plenty of time to discuss both of their hopes and dreams for the future.

"I'll have to clear it with the Alpha first," Brody said, drawing her attention. "I'll talk to Big John first thing tomorrow."

"Do you think he'll object?" Nell bit her lip, looking adorably worried. Brody leaned over to kiss her, then relented once he felt her tension dissolve.

"I'll convince him," he promised her as he drew back to look at her. "You've been here long enough for him to get to know you and your family. I know you can all be trusted, and my counsel counts for a lot with the Alpha. I'm one of his top lieutenants. Which means you'll have a pretty high rank just by virtue of being my mate. Plus, everybody already knows you're a total badass, which means you've already earned some clout of your own." He winked at her, and she frowned.

"Where in the world did you get that idea? I'm no *badass*."

"Are you kidding? That was a direct quote from Lyn after you threw Sig out of your store for coming in stinking of fish guts. You put the fear of Nell into him, and I can tell you Sig doesn't scare easy." Brody was laughing as he remembered the incident. "Sig's a Kodiak when he shifts, which means he's one big-assed bear. Nobody throws him out of anywhere if he doesn't agree. Frankly, we were all pretty glad you told him off because most of us wouldn't have dared tell him to take a shower before he walks around town after one of his week-long fishing trips."

She chuckled, and he laughed with her. It was so easy to be with her. They just...fit.

The Goddess really knew what she was doing when She sent Brody his perfect mate. He had never expected his mate to be human, but he couldn't argue with the Mother of All's wisdom. Nell was perfect for him, and he would do all in his power to be the perfect mate for her.

CHAPTER TEN

Brody talked to John the next morning, and as he'd thought, John had only slight reservations about letting the other Baker girls in on their secret. The Alpha was more than pleased by the news that Brody had taken a mate. A big celebration was being planned to commemorate the mating, which John said he hoped was the first of many in their new community.

But first, Brody had agreed to invite Nell's sisters to dinner at his home, to break the news of their engagement and talk to them privately about his ability to shapeshift. Brody figured a demonstration would be necessary, but he didn't mind putting on a little show for his sisters-in-law, if it would help them accept the truth. He was a bit nervous about how they would react, frankly, and he knew Nell was even more worried.

He'd given her a key to his home and knew she was spending her afternoon, after her shift at the bakery ended, up at their house. She was getting things ready for their family dinner that night, and Brody loved the way she was making herself at home in the den he had built with his future mate in mind. That she liked the place made something inside him stretch with pride. He'd built a house, and now, the Goddess had blessed him with a mate to make it a home.

Everything was going along great until that stupid koala got drunk and started waving a gun around the local pub. Brody had to wade in and break up the standoff, taking a shot in the shoulder before he could wrestle the peashooter away from the drunkard. It wasn't a serious wound, but dragging the koala's drunk ass down to the station and locking him up ate up precious time.

Brody was going to be late to the very important dinner he was supposed to be hosting at his den. Nell wouldn't be happy, and being late wasn't a good way to impress the in-laws either.

There was only one way he'd get there on

time. Straight through the forest.

Brody shrugged out of his bloody uniform and left it on the chair in the back of the jail. Shifting to his bear form, he used one paw to open the back door of the jail and made a beeline through the forest at the back of the building, running on all fours toward his den. He could cover a lot more ground a lot quicker in his fur than if he'd had to drive around the long way on the winding road.

And shifting shape had mostly healed the bullet graze across his arm. He couldn't do much about the blood until he got a chance to clean up, but at least bleeding had stopped with his shift. The only blood left in his fur now was what had been on his body before he'd changed into his grizzly form.

He had left his watch and phone behind at the station, but he thought he might just make it before the sisters arrived. He saw his house and made for the side of it, hoping to sneak in from the deck, shapeshift, and clean up a bit before the girls arrived.

"Brody!" Nell met him in the woods a few yards from the deck, running to him and dropping to her knees to look at his shoulder. "John called and said you'd been shot in the arm. Are you okay?"

She was touching his furry front arm, her hands coming away bloody. There were tears in her eyes, and he knew he had scared her. Dammit. He hadn't meant to worry her.

Brody shifted shape right then and there.

"I'm fine, Nell. It was only a graze, and it healed when I shifted."

"But the blood..." She gestured with her faintly red hands.

"It stopped. Look." He twisted to present his shoulder to her and waited while she touched him gently, probing the area around the wound, wiping away the residual blood with her fingers.

They were both still kneeling on the ground, and he urged her to her feet, taking her into his arms.

"I'm sorry you were scared. John shouldn't have worried you like that." He frowned. The Alpha was going to hear about making Brody's mate cry. The tears in Nell's eyes bothered Brody. A lot.

He rocked her gently in his arms. He was stark naked, but as a werebear, he was used to that after a shift.

"He said you were on your way, but that you'd been shot," she said, tucking her cheek against his chest. She was trembling, so he held her closer. "I didn't listen after that. All I could think of was that you were hurt. Thank God you're okay." She squeezed him tight, making his heart do a little flip at the undeniable evidence of how much she cared. She loosened her hold and moved back a little, meeting his gaze with teary eyes. "You are okay, right? You didn't lose too much blood, did you? And the bullet didn't go in, it just grazed your arm?" She looked at the wound again, as if making sure.

"Yes, I'm fine," he assured her, smiling. "I didn't lose much blood. It was just a scratch, and all evidence of it will be gone by morning. I promise." He moved his hands to her shoulders. "I'm sorry you were worried. And I'm sorry I was almost late for the big dinner." He lifted her off her feet and onto the deck, following close behind. "I need to get cleaned up before your sisters arrive."

"Too late." It was Ashley's voice, coming to him from the far end of the deck.

Looking up quickly, he saw both Ashley and Tina seated at the table with half-full glasses of wine in front of them. They'd been there for some time already.

Dammit. He really was late, after all.

And naked.

Though that didn't bother him as much as it seemed to bother Nell. She'd placed herself strategically in front of him, blocking the sisters' view of his privates, for the most part.

Surprisingly, the sisters didn't look all that alarmed. They had to have seen him shift. He hadn't been all that far away from the deck when he'd changed.

Leaning down beside Nell's ear as she stood with her back to his front, Brody asked, "Do they already know?"

"Oh, you're going to love this," Nell said, turning to face him. The expression on her face was a strange one. She looked sort of angry, but not at him, thank the Goddess. "Apparently, I'm the last one in the family to figure out the big secret of Grizzly Cove. They've known for weeks!" she said in an accusatory tone.

"How?" Brody frowned. Everyone in the cove knew to keep things quiet. If someone had been blabbing, he'd have to have words with them.

"Oh, come on," Tina said, lifting her glass and taking a swallow of the wine. "You guys are terrible at keeping secrets. I saw your brother strip and shift the second day I was in town."

"He shifted in front of you?" Brody was shocked.

"Hello? Roof garden," she sing-songed, rolling her eyes. "We have a hell of a vantage point from up there. I was up there putting the planters together when I saw him getting naked in the woods behind our building. He's kinda hot, so of course I watched. And then, he turned into a freaking bear." Tina downed the rest of the wine and reached for the bottle to refill her glass.

"And he's not the only one we saw from up there," Ashley chimed in. "Nell, did you know that Dr. Olafsson can become a polar bear? He likes to skinny dip, then come up as a bear. And hubba hubba. Doc is built."

"I had no idea you two were such voyeurs," Nell said over her shoulder. She seemed more hurt than mad. Brody put his hands on her shoulders, stroking gently, hoping to soothe his mate. He didn't like seeing her upset.

"See?" Tina said in an accusing tone. "That's exactly why we didn't tell you." Tina drank more wine. "You would have totally spoiled our fun."

"Can you believe them?" Nell said, moving more into Brody's arms. "And here I was all worried about how we were going to tell them. I agonized over this big revelation, and it turns out I'm the only one who was in the dark."

Brody tried to think of the best response. "Well, at least now you know they're not going to run screaming into the night at the idea there are shapeshifters in the world."

He tried giving her a lopsided smile, and she responded with a faint one of her own. He felt relief flow through him. She was recovering from both the shock of hearing he'd been shot and from learning that her sisters had known about the town's secret all along and neglected to tell her.

"Ashley, Tina, we wanted to tell you that we're getting married." He let that announcement fall without waiting for a response. There would be time for congratulations later. First, he had to get some pants on and comfort his mate—not necessarily in that order. "Now, if you'll please excuse us for a few minutes, we'll be right back," he said firmly, as he walked slowly backwards into the house, Nell still in his arms. The sisters watched but didn't move from their seats on the deck.

Once inside, he couldn't wait. He had to take her into his arms. He had to comfort her and hold her. The bear inside him demanded he make her happy again, and Brody could do no less than agree.

He dipped his head and claimed her lips in a gentle kiss that quickly turned into something much hotter.

"Way to go, sis," Ashley called from the other side of the screen door while Tina let out a wolf whistle. Brody paid them no heed. He was way too busy kissing his mate.

# # #

EXCERPT:
MATING DANCE
Grizzly Cove #2

CHAPTER ONE

Tom Masdan was the one and only lawyer in Grizzly Cove, Washington, and he liked it that way. Tom figured if there was more than one lawyer in a town, they were obligated to fight things out in court, which is one aspect of his profession that he loathed. The conflict of the adversarial process annoyed his inner bear and made him want to scratch, claw and just beat his opponent into submission rather than wait to hear what some old guy wearing a dress and sitting on a podium had to say.

Tom thought, not for the first time, that maybe studying law hadn't been the brightest idea he'd ever had. Then again, shifters needed legal representation every once in awhile, just like everybody else. That's where he came in.

He enjoyed helping people like himself—people who lived under the radar of the human population. Shapeshifters had to learn to adapt to the modern, human world. That included following the laws of the countries in which they lived.

Tom had been born and raised in the United States. He'd gone to an ivy league law school back east. Since then, he had offered his services solely to the *were* of North America, or any foreign-based *were* that needed legal representation in the States. He filed claims, did a lot of paperwork, and helped shapeshifters of all kinds create the paper trail that humans found so necessary to their existence.

In his job, he had traveled all over, but had never found the one woman who could complete him. He'd never found his mate.

So when his long-time friend, John Marshall—known simply as Big John to most folks—proposed the idea of forming their own little enclave on the Washington coast, and putting out an open call for any bear shifters who wanted to move there,

Tom was cautiously optimistic. The idea of gathering a relatively large group of usually solitary bears in one town was both novel and intriguing. It could also be dangerous as hell, but Tom trusted Big John's ultra-Alpha tendencies to keep everybody in line.

John had asked Tom to begin the process of turning the large, adjoining parcels of real estate John had bought over the past several years, into a new town. There were lots of forms to file with the state of Washington, and quite a few building contracts to oversee. He'd also overseen the real estate deals of neighboring properties for each of the core group of bear shifters that had joined John on this quest. It had taken a good portion of the last several years of Tom's life, but the town of Grizzly Cove had finally become a reality.

It was a really good reality too. The town was small by human standards, but already a few dozen bear shifters had answered John's call for settlers. There were still more males than females, but with the recent decision to allow a few, select, human-owned businesses to open up on Main Street, things were beginning to change.

Just last week, the sheriff had found his

mate in the human woman who, along with her two sisters, owned the new bake shop. It was a true mating, and Tom was happy for them.

But, it had become clear, that the so-called secret of Grizzly Cove hadn't really been that much of the secret to the other two sisters. They'd taken the news about shapeshifters, in stride. It seemed they'd already figured it out.

Which meant that the shifter residents weren't being careful enough. And that the two remaining sisters needed to agree not to spill the beans.

A job for Tom, the Alpha had said. Tom wasn't so sure. He might be a lawyer, but he wasn't necessarily a smooth talker. He did his best work on a computer, in an office. He wasn't the kind of attorney who schmoozed clients over three martini lunches.

But Big John had asked him to try, so there he was, approaching the bakery he had never stepped foot in before. It wasn't that he was shy. It was more that he hadn't really wanted to interact with the new humans in town, until the experiment had been proven a success. The bakery was the first of many applications Tom had received from business people who wanted to open stores in their town.

The decision had been made to allow the bakery—and the three sisters—as a trial run. Their food was excellent, from all accounts, and most of the shifters in town liked the women, and were glad one of their comrades had found a mate.

Humans made decent mates and bears couldn't be picky. There weren't a lot of bear shifters in the first place, and it wasn't uncommon for them to find mates outside their species. A lot of bear shifters took human mates.

It didn't diminish the magic. Bears had more than most shifters, and Tom often thought, that's why they were kind of rare. But what did he know? Only the Mother of All—the Goddess who watched over all shifters—knew for certain.

The bell over the door tinkled as Tom pushed into the bakery. Immediately, he was surrounded by the most scrumptious scents of baking bread, honey, and some kind of cheese. He took stock of the place and realized he was the only customer this early in the day. Only one of the sisters was there, working in the back.

That would be the middle sister, he'd been told. She worked the morning shift and her name was Ashley Baker. The irony of the Baker sisters owning a bakery had struck Tom as suspicious when he'd first seen their application, but he'd done thorough background checks on all three women and they really were named Baker, and had been since their birth.

The blonde woman came out from behind one of the ovens, wiping her hands on her apron as she greeted him. She took up her position behind the counter with a brisk sort of efficiency and Tom was struck momentarily dumb when she smiled.

"Good morning," she said brightly. "What can I get for you?"

Sonuva… Tom's bear sat up and wanted to roar. It liked the woman.

Hell, it more than *liked* her. It was thinking *mate*.

No. Way.

To read more, get your copy of
Mating Dance *by Bianca D'Arc.*

ABOUT THE AUTHOR

Bianca D'Arc has run a laboratory, climbed the corporate ladder in the shark-infested streets of lower Manhattan, studied and taught martial arts, and earned the right to put a whole bunch of letters after her name, but she's always enjoyed writing more than any of her other pursuits. She grew up and still lives on Long Island, where she keeps busy with an extensive garden, several aquariums full of very demanding fish, and writing her favorite genres of paranormal, fantasy and sci-fi romance.

Bianca loves to hear from readers and can be reached through Twitter (@BiancaDArc), Facebook (BiancaDArcAuthor) or through the various links on her website.

WELCOME TO THE D'ARC SIDE…
WWW.BIANCADARC.COM

OTHER BOOKS
BY BIANCA D'ARC

Paranormal Romance

Brotherhood of Blood
One & Only
Rare Vintage
Phantom Desires
Sweeter Than Wine
Forever Valentine
Wolf Hills*
Wolf Quest

Tales of the Were
Lords of the Were
Inferno

Tales of the Were ~ The Others
Rocky
Slade

Tales of the Were ~ Redstone Clan
The Purrfect Stranger
Grif
Red
Magnus
Bobcat
Matt

Tales of the Were ~ String of Fate
Cat's Cradle
King's Throne
Jacob's Ladder
Her Warriors

Tales of the Were ~ Grizzly Cove
All About the Bear
Mating Dance
Night Shift
Alpha Bear
Saving Grace

Guardians of the Dark
Half Past Dead
Once Bitten, Twice Dead
A Darker Shade of Dead
The Beast Within
Dead Alert

Gifts of the Ancients: Warrior's Heart

Epic Fantasy Erotic Romance

Dragon Knights
Maiden Flight*
The Dragon Healer
Border Lair
Master at Arms

Dragon Knights
(continued)
The Ice Dragon**
Prince of Spies***
Wings of Change
FireDrake
Dragon Storm
Keeper of the Flame
Hidden Dragons
Sea Dragon

Science Fiction Romance

StarLords
Hidden Talent
Talent For Trouble
Shy Talent

Jit'Suku Chronicles ~ Arcana
King of Swords
King of Cups
King of Clubs
King of Stars
End of the Line

Jit'Suku Chronicles ~ Sons of Amber
Angel in the Badlands

Futuristic Erotic Romance

Resonance Mates
Hara's Legacy**
Davin's Quest
Jaci's Experiment
Grady's Awakening
Harry's Sacrifice

* RT Book Reviews Awards Nominee
** EPPIE Award Winner
*** CAPA Award Winner

WWW.BIANCADARC.COM

Made in the USA
Middletown, DE
27 April 2017